Thomas Takes a Vacation

Cover art by Jim Durk

A GOLDEN BOOK • NEW YORK
Thomas the Tank Engine & Friends™
CREATED BY BRITT ALLCROFT
Based on The Railway Series by The Reverend W Awdry.
© 2015 Gullane (Thomas LLC).
Thomas the Tank Engine & Friends and Thomas & Friends are trademarks of Gullane (Thomas) Limited.
HIT and the HIT Entertainment logo are trademarks of HIT Entertainment Limited.
All rights reserved. Published in the United States by Golden Books, an imprint of Random House Children's
Books, a division of Random House LLC, 1745 Broadway, New York, NY 10019, and in Canada by Random House
of Canada Limited, Toronto, Penguin Random House Companies. Golden Books, A Golden Book, and the
G colophon are registered trademarks of Random House LLC.
ISBN 978-0-553-50846-8
randomhousekids.com
www.thomasandfriends.com
Printed in the United States of America
10 9 8 7 6 5 4 3 2 1

HIT entertainment

Thomas is a Really Useful Engine.

He works hard every day.

Day in . . .

and day out.

Thomas is ready to work, even in the rain!

Connect the dots to make an umbrella,
so Sir Topham Hatt can stay dry.

And, of course, Thomas works when the sun shines.

Thomas is always ready to do the job!

Some days are busier than others.

After one busy week, Sir Topham Hatt tells Thomas to take a vacation.

Thomas asks Sir Topham Hatt where he should go.

Thomas asks Percy what he thinks.

Thomas asks James for advice, too.

Thomas wonders if Whiff has a suggestion.

Thomas asks both Edward and Henry for ideas.

**Maybe Thomas will take a
bird-watching trip.**

Thomas can see pretty birds everywhere on Sodor.

And ducks (and Bertie), too.

Thomas thinks about taking a voyage across the ocean.

He could see windmills in Holland.

Or watch artists painting in France.

Thomas imagines riding through mountain tunnels in Switzerland.

He thinks about rolling through green fields all over England.

He could visit castles in Wales.

Find the castle that's different from the others. Then color them all.

Thomas even thinks about chuffing through pine forests in faraway America!

But staying home is nice, too. Thomas likes the Island of Sodor, because . . .

there are friendly families to visit.

And people everywhere are always happy to see Thomas.

Draw a kite for Thomas' little friend.

Visiting the Duke and Duchess of Boxford at their lovely summerhouse on Sodor is nice.

Bertie is always happy to have a race with Thomas.

Follow the lines to see who wins the race to the station.

Thomas and Percy like sharing the news of the day.

Thomas likes saying hi to Harold as he hovers over the countryside.

Alfie is always happy to have a little chat.

It's fun when Thomas visits his friend the Rocket at Ulfstead Castle.

Thomas likes to peep "hello" as he passes a cow in the meadow.

Thomas is happy to see his animal friends— even in a rainstorm.

And there's always a rainbow when the sun shines again.

Neville thinks Thomas should just rest at Tidmouth Sheds.

Instead, Thomas keeps right on rolling around Sodor.

Finish this hot air balloon floating above Thomas.

Where, oh where, will Thomas take a vacation? He can't decide!

Thomas thinks and thinks about it.

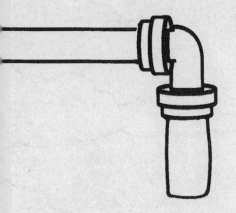

Then one day, Thomas and Belle puff along the seashore.

Thomas thinks it might be nice to relax by the water.

But Thomas thinks that the river is a little too quiet.

Brendam Docks is on the water,
but it's too busy.

When Thomas passes the lighthouse, an idea flies into his funnel!

Draw a circle around the places Thomas *doesn't* think about for his vacation.

While he helps Percy with a Special Delivery, Thomas makes up his mind.

Thomas decides to take a vacation by the seaside.

Sir Topham Hatt agrees that this is a fine idea.

He tells Thomas to relax by the beach.

Sir Topham Hatt also has a gift for Thomas' driver—he's going on vacation, too!

Draw Thomas' driver.

Thomas stops on his way to let Spencer go by.

When Thomas sees some seagulls, he knows he's getting close!

Draw a boat racing Thomas to th
Add some waves, too.

At last, Thomas is on vacation!
Have a good time, Thomas!